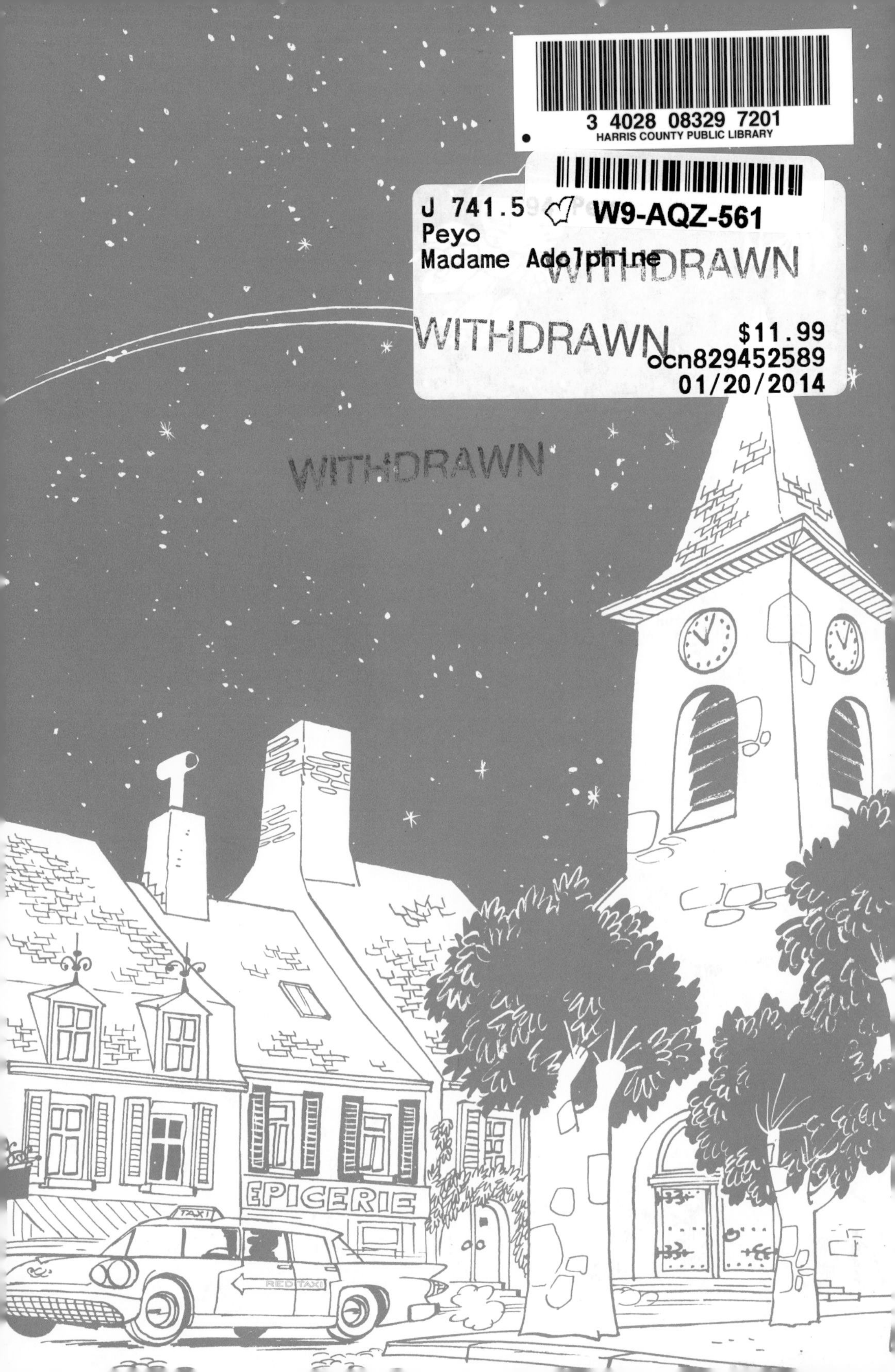
EPICERIE
TAXI
RED TAXI

BENNY BREAKIRON

IN

MADAME ADOLPHINE

BY

Peyo

WITH BACKGROUNDS BY *WILL*

PAPERCUTZ™

NEW YORK

 **GRAPHIC NOVELS AVAILABLE FROM PAPERCUT𝗭**™

BENNY BREAKIRON

1. **THE RED TAXIS**
2. **MADAME ADOLPHINE**
3. **TWELVE TRIALS OF BENNY BREAKIRON** (COMING SOON)

THE SMURFS

1. **THE PURPLE SMURFS**
2. **THE SMURFS AND THE MAGIC FLUTE**
3. **THE SMURF KING**
4. **THE SMURFETTE**
5. **THE SMURFS AND THE EGG**
6. **THE SMURFS AND THE HOWLIBIRD**
7. **THE ASTROSMURF**
8. **THE SMURF APPRENTICE**
9. **GARGAMEL AND THE SMURFS**
10. **THE RETURN OF THE SMURFETTE**
11. **THE SMURF OLYMPICS**
12. **SMURF VS. SMURF**
13. **SMURF SOUP**
14. **THE BABY SMURF**
15. **THE SMURFLINGS**

BENNY BREAKIRON graphic novels are available in hardcover only for $11.99 each. THE SMURFS graphic novels are available in paperback for $5.99 each and in hardcover for $10.99 each at booksellers everywhere. You can also order online at www.papercutz.com. Or call 1-800-886-1223, Monday through Friday, 9 – 5 EST. MC, Visa, and AmEx accepted. To order by mail, please add $4.00 for postage and handling for first book ordered, $1.00 for each additional book and make check payable to NBM Publishing. Send to: Papercutz, 160 Broadway, Suite 700, East Wing, New York, NY 10038.

BENNY BREAKIRON and THE SMURFS graphic novels are also available digitally wherever e-books are sold.

WWW. PAPERCUTZ.COM

BENNY BREAKIRON
#2 "Madame Adolphine"

© Peyo – 2013 - Licensed through Lafig Belgium - www.smurf.com

English Translation Copyright © 2013 by Papercutz.
All rights reserved.

Joe Johnson, *TRANSLATION*
Adam Grano, *DESIGN AND PRODUCTION*
Janice Chiang, *LETTERING*
Matt. Murray, *SMURF CONSULTANT*
Beth Scorzato, *PRODUCTION COORDINATOR*
Michael Petranek, *ASSOCIATE EDITOR*
Jim Salicrup
EDITOR-IN-CHIEF

ISBN: 978-1-59707-436-0

Papercutz books may be purchased for business or promotional use. For information on bulk purchases please contact Macmillan Corporate and Premium Sales Department at (800) 221-7945 x5442.

PRINTED IN CHINA
SEPTEMBER 2013 BY NEW ERA PRINTING LTD.
UNIT C, 8F, WORLDWIDE CENTRE
123 TUNG CHAU STREET, HONG KONG

DISTRIBUTED BY MACMILLAN
FIRST PAPERCUTZ PRINTING

MADAME ADOLPHINE

Vivejoie-la-Grande, a cute, little city with provincial charm, that's where Benny Breakiron lives.

This day, his homework finished, he is going to meet his friends at the Jules Petty Square...

MEEOW

?

MEEOW!

Oh! The poor, little cat! He can't get down!

Here, kitty! Come on! Here! Don't be afraid! I'll catch you! Come quick!

It's no use!

The street's deserted! What if I--

Has anyone told you about Benny? He's a very strong, little boy...

One... two...

...INCREDIBLY STRONG!

?

?

Three!
>Hmf!<

KRAK

!

MELANIE!

Voilà!

Now I have to put this tree back like it was... You should always put your things away...

...That's what the school teacher said!

SPROTCH

There! And now, go home quickly and no more climbing trees!

But no, Melanie, I haven't been drinking! I swear to you I saw the tree fall on the street! You'll see! You'll see!

Yes, I do see! **I MOSTLY SEE THAT SOMEONE'S PULLING MY LEG HERE!**

But-- but, Melanie, I-- I swear to you that--

2

BONJOUR! JOHN-JOHN! PETER!

HEY! WHERE ARE YOU?

They must be at the sandbox... or at the music stand...

No!... They're not there!

Pardon, Monsieur, you haven't seen my friends, have you? You know, the big one with freckles and the one with glasses.

No, Benny! I haven't seen them!

Well, zut!... But they'd told me they'd come today!

What will I do now?

I really wanted to play "Cowboys and Indians"!...

Hello, little boy! What's your name?

Benny, Madame!

Oh? That's a lovely name!... I'm Adolphine!

Ah?... Uh... that's a nice name, too.

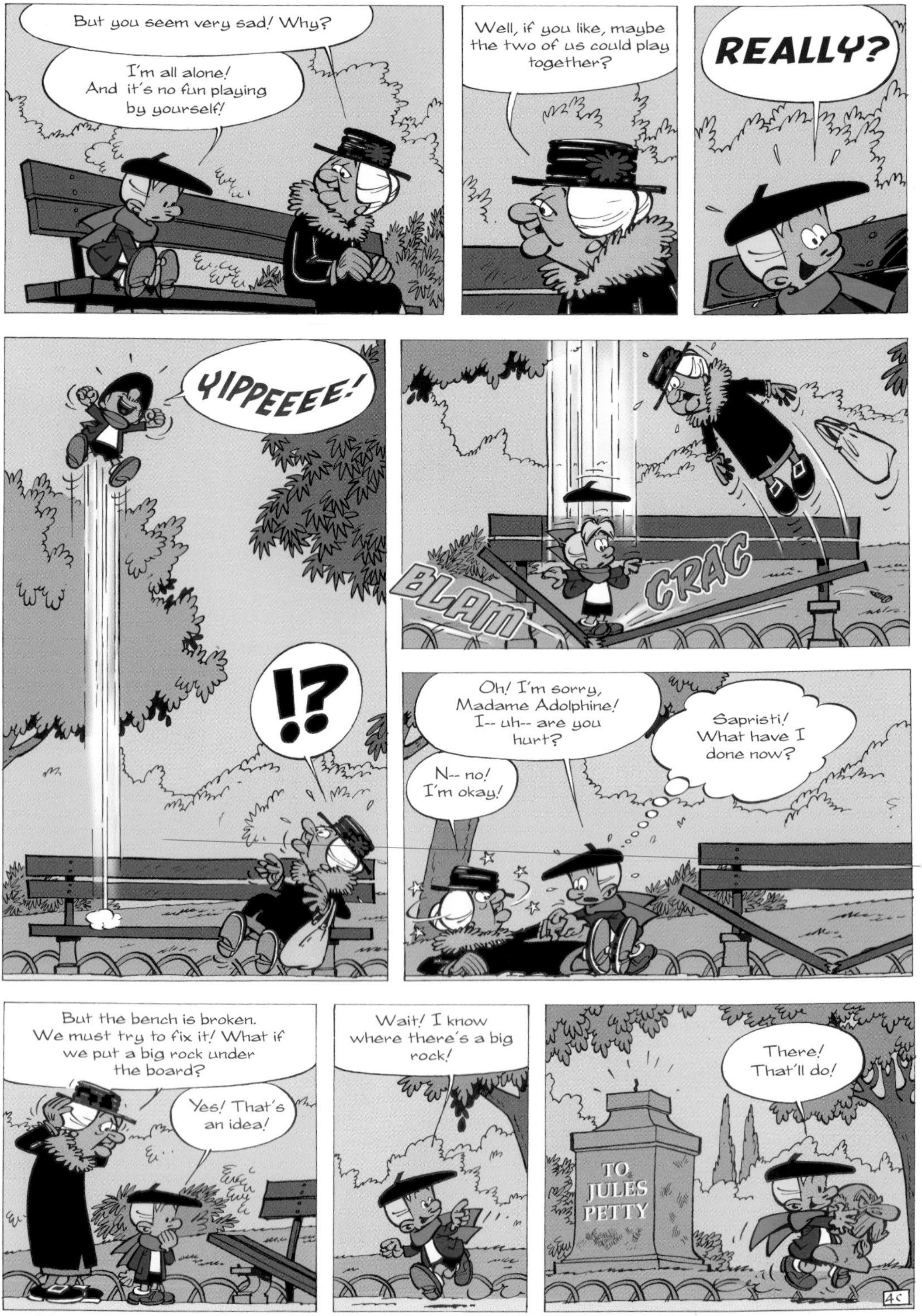
But you seem very sad! Why?
I'm all alone! And it's no fun playing by yourself!
Well, if you like, maybe the two of us could play together?
REALLY?
YIPPEEEE!
BLAM
CRAC
!?
Oh! I'm sorry, Madame Adolphine! I-- uh-- are you hurt?
Sapristi! What have I done now?
N-- no! I'm okay!
But the bench is broken. We must try to fix it! What if we put a big rock under the board?
Yes! That's an idea!
Wait! I know where there's a big rock!
There! That'll do!
TO JULES PETTY
4C

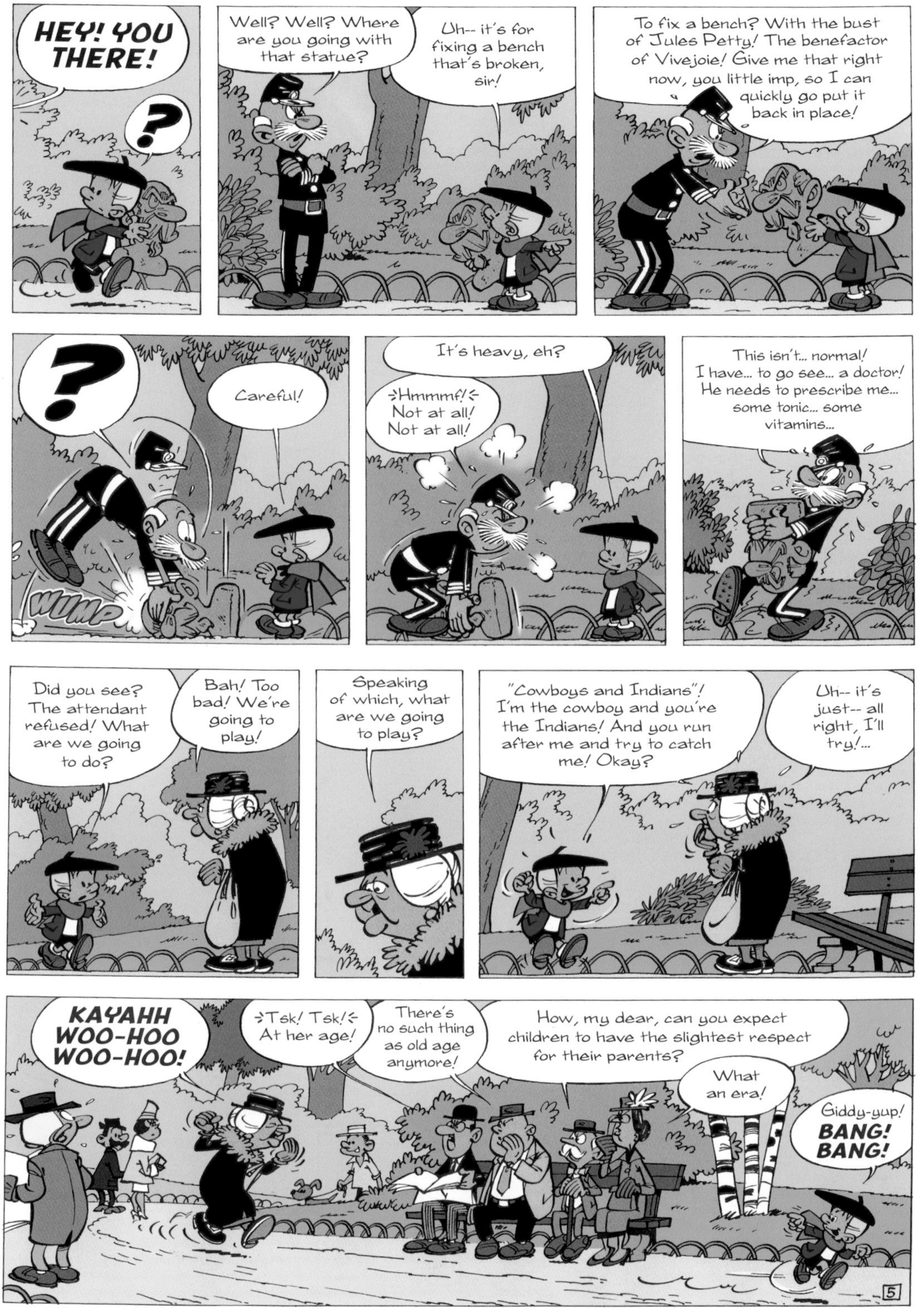

HEY! YOU THERE!
?
Well? Well? Where are you going with that statue?
Uh-- it's for fixing a bench that's broken, sir!
To fix a bench? With the bust of Jules Petty! The benefactor of Vivejoie! Give me that right now, you little imp, so I can quickly go put it back in place!
?
Careful!
WUMP
It's heavy, eh?
Hmmmf! Not at all! Not at all!
This isn't... normal! I have... to go see... a doctor! He needs to prescribe me... some tonic... some vitamins...
Did you see? The attendant refused! What are we going to do?
Bah! Too bad! We're going to play!
Speaking of which, what are we going to play?
"Cowboys and Indians"! I'm the cowboy and you're the Indians! And you run after me and try to catch me! Okay?
Uh-- it's just-- all right, I'll try!...
KAYAHH WOO-HOO WOO-HOO!
Tsk! Tsk! At her age!
There's no such thing as old age anymore!
How, my dear, can you expect children to have the slightest respect for their parents?
What an era!
Giddy-yup! BANG! BANG!
5

Poor Madame Adolphine! She doesn't run very fast! I'll let her catch up!

There! Gotcha!

Oww! I've been caught!

⇉Whew!⇇ Running like that makes you thirsty! Would you like to have some lemonade?

Oh! Yes, there's a drink stand over there!

One lemonade, please, Madame!

Madame Adolphine's nice!

Aren't you drinking anything?

Me? Oh! No... I can't anyhow!

Oh? Why not?

Uh... because... I... well... I'll explain it to you one day!

DONG DONG

Oh! It's already six o'clock! I have to go home!

We had fun, didn't we? Will you come to the park again?

I don't know! I'll try!

God will reward you a hundred times over, my good lady!

Madame Adolphine has a kind heart!

Voilà! I've arrived! I live over there in the last house!...

Well, goodbye, Benny!

Au revoir, Madame Adolphine! And merci!

It's noth-- no-- no-- ⇉wooo⇇ ...⇉sticlop⇇ ... ⇉tchasblooblib⇇ ...

?

8

EH?!

SWOOSH

MADAME ADOLPHINE! MADAME ADOLPHINE! ANSWER ME!

It's no use! She's fainted!... I can't leave here like this on the sidewalk!

I'll put her in the living room!

There! Don't get upset! It won't be serious!... I'll take care of you!

There must be a little book in the medicine cabinet that says what should be done in the event of an accident!

Ah! Here it is!

Wounds... electrocution... poisoning... Ah! Fainting!

Uh... symptoms: cold sweats, a pale face, a weak pulse, but rapid!...

!

But-- but her pulse isn't beating at all?!

9

A doctor! Quick! A doctor!

Hello? Is that you, Doctor?... This is Benny Breakiron! There's an elderly lady on the chair whom I met at the park, whose pulse isn't beating now and who fainted on the sidewalk and who's here, now, and I read in the book that says that... yes!... Okay! I'll wait for you, Doctor!

The doctor's going to come right away! And he's going to cure you, you'll see! The doctor's a very nice man!

RIINNG

Ah! That's him!

Well? Where's that lady?

In the living room, Doctor!

All right! Wait for me here!

Poor Madame Adolphine! She was so nice!

THAT'S SHAMEFUL! SOMEONE'S MAKING FUN OF ME! BUT THEY WON'T GET AWAY WITH IT!

?

I, too, played pranks when I was little! On grocers! On butchers! But **NEVER** on doctors!

But--

SLAM

But I--

But what could have happened?

She's still not moving! So why did the doctor get angry?... I don't understand what's going on!

What am I going to do now? If only I knew her address!...

You know, she must have some identity cards!... Let's see, a change-purse... a handkerchief... a comb... no! There aren't any!

Oh? A phone number!... What if I tried that?...

Hello? Uh-- excuse me, monsieur, but I found your number in the shopping bag of an elderly lady who's at my home and who-- yes, Madame Adolphine!... Do you know her?

Yes, of course! I was wondering, in fact, where she'd gotten off to! Tell her to come home and to-- ah?-- And she's not moving any longer?... Okay! Give me your address!... Yes!... All right! I'll be at your place in two minutes!

And two minutes later...

Good evening! I've come to get Adolphine!

Yes, come in!

Here she is! She's still not moving!

Bah! I'll take care of her. And tomorrow she'll dance around like silly!

Well? Aren't you ashamed, you wicked girl? Still running away at your age! Next time I'll lock you in the basement! That'll teach you!...

Come on! Let's go! We're going home!

11

M'sieur! Wait! Her hat fell off!

Ah? Thanks!

CAREFUL!

BAM

Oh! I'm sorry!... Luckily nothing's wrong with the door!

!

Let's go! Into the car, Fifi!

What's he doing? Surely he isn't going to put her in the trunk, I hope?...

WUMP

NO!

Ah! Her hat and her bag! So that's it!... Good evening, my boy! And thanks for calling me!

What a brute!

Well! I hope that wicked man's telling the truth and will cure her! Madame Adolphine is so nice!

The next day...

So, the fellow threw her in the trunk and took off!

And then...?

Afterwards? That's it! I went to bed!

Ah! No! You have to tell me the end!

But this isn't some story I'm making up! It really happened!

That's not true! I don't believe you!

What's more, you're always telling jokes! It's like the day when you told me you were strong, that you could lift huge weights, jump higher than a house, and run faster than a car!

But that's true!

Liar! When I asked you to prove it to me, you couldn't!

I had a cold! And I when I have a cold, I lose all my strength!

Nice excuse! Now Joey, that's a boy who's strong! Do you know what Joey does in class?

No!

He drinks from INKWELLS!

!

Çà Alors! Come quick!

WHA--?

I'm going to prove to you I'm not a liar!

13

MADAME ADOLPHINE!

?

Ah! I'm so happy to see you! You're doing better now?

Uh-- why yes, little boy! But--

You sure did give me a scare yesterday! For a moment, I thought you were dead!

Me?...

Excuse me, but I don't understand what you mean! For starters, who are you?

What? You don't recognize me?...

Goodness, no! I've never seen you!

!?

But-- I'm Benny! Benny Breakiron!... I met you yesterday at the Jules Petty Square! We played "Cowboys and Indians" together!...

12 A

No! You must be mistaken! I was at my cousin's yesterday and I only returned to Vivejoie this morning!

But-- it's not possible! I--

You must be confusing me with another old lady!... Here! Have a piece of candy to make you feel better!

But--

LIAR!

But, but, I swear to you that-- Wait! Listen!...

I don't understand anything anymore!... Nothing at all!

12

14

I wasn't dreaming though! There was a man who came to get Madame Adolphine last night!... If only I knew where he lives...

But, in fact--

What did I do with that paper?

Ah! Voilà!

They can give me the address at the Post Office!

Pardon, M'sieur, could you give me the name and address of the gentleman who has this phone number?

Monsieur Vladlavodka, at 18 Horseshoe Street!

Ah! It's here!

Monsieur Vladlavodka, please, Madame?

He's in his workshop back there, in the rear of the courtyard!

Nobody's answering? It's because he's in the backroom! Go on in!

!

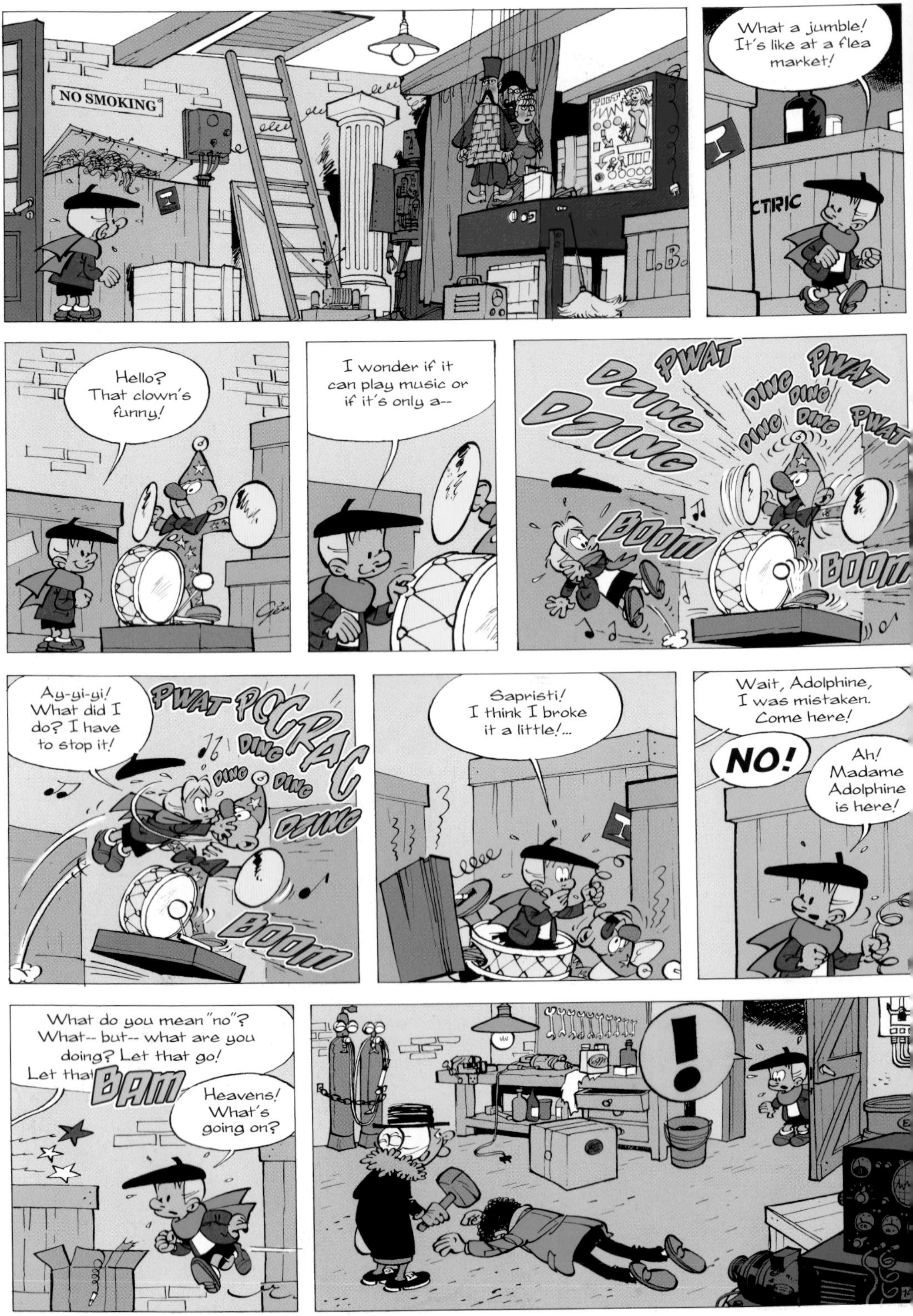
NO SMOKING
What a jumble! It's like at a flea market!
CTRIC
Hello? That clown's funny!
I wonder if it can play music or if it's only a--
PWAT
PWAT
DZING
DZING
DING DING DING DING
PWAT
BOOM
BOOM
Ay-yi-yi! What did I do? I have to stop it!
PWAT
POCRAC
DING
DING
DING
DZING
BOOM
Sapristi! I think I broke it a little!...
Wait, Adolphine, I was mistaken. Come here!
NO!
Ah! Madame Adolphine is here!
What do you mean "no"? What-- but-- what are you doing? Let that go! Let that
BAM
Heavens! What's going on?
!

Why it's little Benny! How are you, you rascal?

Madame Adolphine! What did you do?

Oh! Nothing! That fellow was bothering me. So, bing, I gave him a little knock on the head!

But that's terrible! We have to treat him! Where is there some water?

Forget about it! He'll wake up on his own! Let's take this chance to get the heck out of here!

To get the what--?!

To skedaddle!... To vamoose, if you prefer!

Only we got to do so fast, before the fellow wakes up!... Are you coming?

Why, no! That's impossible! I--

Okay! Stay put, if you like! See you later!

What awful language! But she didn't talk like that before!... What happened?

Oww! My head!

Ah! He's waking up!

Ohhhh!·

Are you hurt? Do you want me to call a doctor?

What?... Hey! I recognize you! You're the one who called me yesterday to tell me that Adolphine--

ADOLPHINE! WHERE'S ADOLPHINE?

15

17

Uh-- Madame Adolphine has left, M'sieur!

LEFT?!

Oh, good heavens! I've got to get her back here at all costs!

...Before she causes some calamity!

Blast it! She's not even in the street now!

Quick! Let's jump in the car! She mustn't be far away!

Heh heh heh! I fooled them! I fooled them!

Heh heh heh!

Who knows what she's capable of now?!... And all because I stupidly mixed up my circuits!

Huh?

Oh, yes! And now her electronic system is out of whack! Do you understand?

Uh-- no! Madame Adolphine has an electronic system?...

Why of course! She's a robot!

!

Are you kidding me?... Madame Adolphine isn't a robot!...

Is too!

Come on now! I've seen robots before! They're big contraptions made all of iron, with tons of buttons on their bellies and antennas on their heads!

Their eyes are bulbs that turn on and off, and they're incredibly strong! What's more, there was one last year at the department store on the market square! It was handing out leaflets!

I know! I'm the one who built it!

Oh?

Yes! I'm a robot-builder and I'm interested in electronics! For some time, I've had the idea of building a robot! But not like the other ones!...

I want it to resemble us in every respect! For it to walk, talk, see, hear, remember, exactly like you and me! It was possible thanks to immense progress that's been made in cybernetics these past few years.

In what?

In cybernetics! It's a science whose goal is the study of mechanisms capable of operating themselves!

Have you ever heard of Grey Walter's famous tortoises?

Uh-- no. What's special about them?

They're electronic! They react to light and possess an actual memory! If, for example, their batteries are running down, they plug themselves into an electrical outlet to recharge them!

So, in short, I started building my robot! I made an old woman out of it because it was easier to hide all the equipment under long clothes! What's more, the slightly jerky gait and gestures of a robot were better suited to an older person!

A few days ago, stuffed with miles of wires, transistors, motors, photoelectric cells, etc., Adolphine took her first steps! She was programmed to be gentle, kindly--

Oh! Yes-- Madame Adolphine is nice!

She **WAS** nice! For, alas, while repairing her, I made a mistake and reversed two circuits! And now, Adolphine is **MEAN!**

Meanwhile, that's three times I've done a tour of the neighborhood and I still don't see her! Let's return to the workshop. Maybe she came back there!

No! She isn't here!

There's nothing to be done! I'll wait for her here! Maybe she'll come back when night falls! Go on home, little buddy, it's getting late!...

Yes, M'sieur!

A robot! Madame Adolphine! I can't get over it!

But then--

Now I understand why I didn't feel her pulse beating! And why the doctor got angry! Hee hee hee hee!

DINGALINGALING

See you tomorrow, Madame Adolphine!

!

That's her! This is my chance!

BEUR
FR

Madame Adolphine!

Oh, you again?

Come quick! You must return to the workshop to repair your circuits, otherwise you'll keep being mean!

WHAT?!

I know you're a robot! Monsieur Vladlavodka told me so! Come on, let's go! He'll fix you, and you'll be nice again!

But-- but what are you telling me?!

Be good and give me your hand and come! Otherwise, I'll have to bring you by force!

Let me go! Help!

Too bad! You asked for it!

HELP!

18

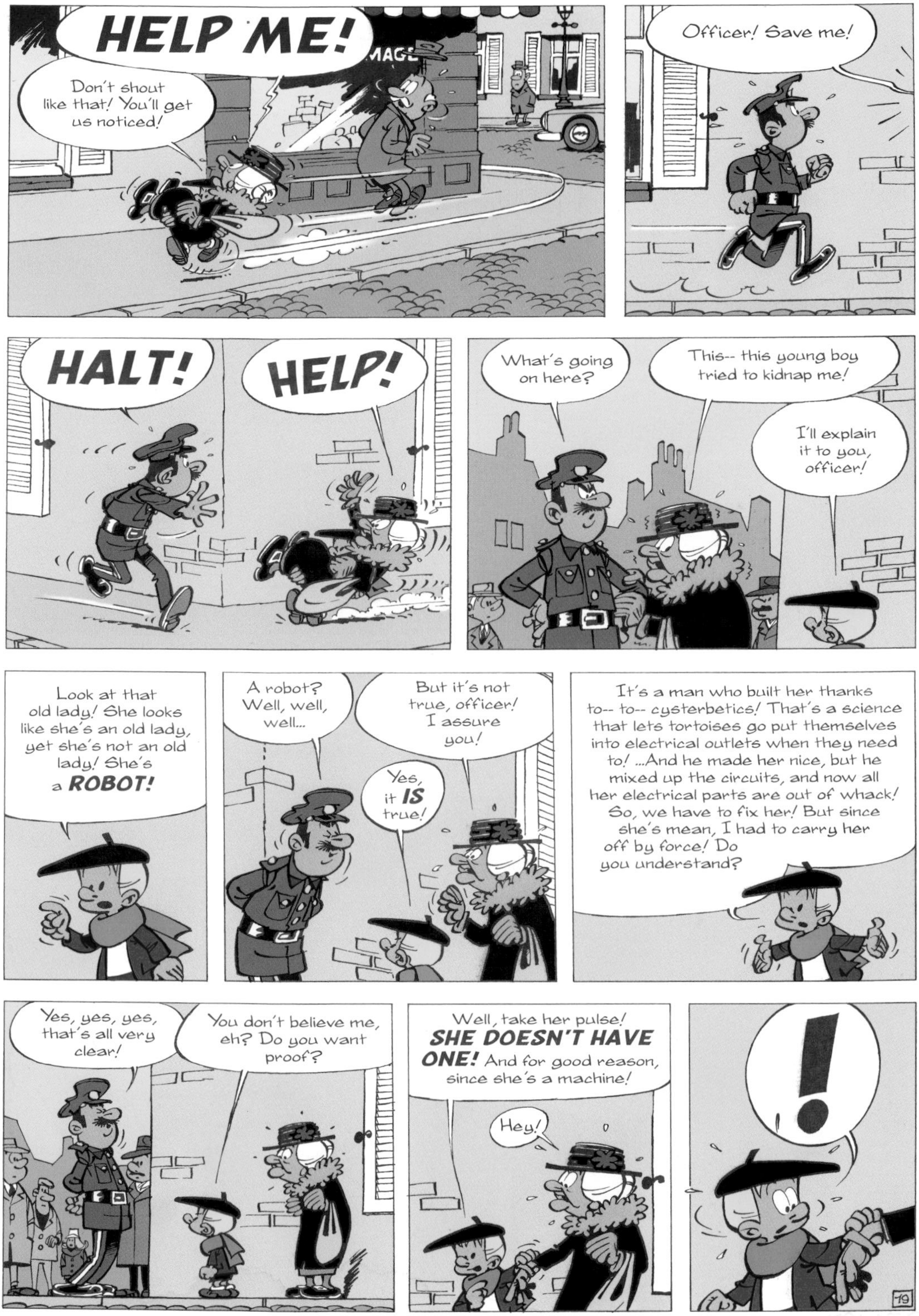
HELP ME!
Don't shout like that! You'll get us noticed!
Officer! Save me!
HALT!
HELP!
What's going on here?
This-- this young boy tried to kidnap me!
I'll explain it to you, officer!
Look at that old lady! She looks like she's an old lady, yet she's not an old lady! She's a ROBOT!
A robot? Well, well, well...
But it's not true, officer! I assure you!
Yes, it IS true!
It's a man who built her thanks to-- to-- cysterbetics! That's a science that lets tortoises go put themselves into electrical outlets when they need to! ...And he made her nice, but he mixed up the circuits, and now all her electrical parts are out of whack! So, we have to fix her! But since she's mean, I had to carry her off by force! Do you understand?
Yes, yes, yes, that's all very clear!
You don't believe me, eh? Do you want proof?
Well, take her pulse! SHE DOESN'T HAVE ONE! And for good reason, since she's a machine!
Hey!
!
19

But-- but your pulse is **BEATING!?**

Of course! Otherwise I'd be dead!

But then... you-- you're not a robot?!

No! I'm an old lady in flesh and blood! Who told you I was a robot?

It was Mister Vladlavodka! I thought that-- uh-- well-- I don't know what to say, Madame Adolphine! I--

It's all right! Forget about it! Here, take this candy and go home quickly!

What a mess! Why did Mister Vladlavodka tell me she was a robot?

Ah? Is he making fun of me? Well, we'll see about that!

Why did you lie to me? Madame Adolphine isn't a robot!

What?!

Yes, she **IS** a robot!

That's not true! I found her and I felt her pulse beating! And a robot doesn't have a pulse!

But-- good heavens, I understand! I bet you met Madame Adolphine!

!?

20

But-- yes, I did meet her! I just now told you so!

Okay! But the one that you saw isn't my robot! That's the real Madame Adolphine!

?

I'll explain! For my robot to look real, I'd decided to make an exact copy of an elderly lady living in the neighborhood: Madame Adolphine! With the help of photos taken unbeknownst to her, I managed to reproduce her face, her clothes, her look! And that's why there are two Madame Adolphine's now: a real one and a fake! Do you understand?

Meanwhile, my own Adolphine still hasn't come back! I wonder where she could be?

Yes, in fact, what has become of Madame Adolphine in the meantime?... The fake one!

ARMS AND AMMUNITION

ARMS AND AMMUNITION

ARMS AND AMMUNITION

Hello, sir! I'd like a revolver!

Certainly, Madame! I'll show you what we have!

SIMPLEX-C

Here's a practical, sturdy little model that'll give you much satisfaction!

Is it loaded?

Yes! Be careful! I've put a bullet in the barrel!

Good! Hands in the air, then, big man, or I'll take you out!

!

ARMS AND AMMUNITION

23

A few moments later...

The bank? It's the big building over there, at the end of that street!

BANK OF THE S.O.C.I.S.

BANG BANG BANG

Hey! Taxi!

Where do I take you, my good lady?

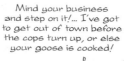

Mind your business and step on it!... I've got to get out of town before the cops turn up, or else your goose is cooked!

Is-- is this a joke? You--

Shut up and drive!

VROOM

The next morning...

DRRRING
DRRRING

Hello? Ah! It's you, Mister Vladlavodka? Well? Has Madame Adolphine come back?... No?... Do you have any news of her? What's that?..............

WHAT?

--And luckily, she didn't hurt anyone! Next, it seems she jumped into a cab and made the driver drive her out of town! She made him get out there and she drove off with the car!...

Are you certain it was really her?... Yes!... Yes, of course!... In that case, I think we must inform the police that the woman they're searching for is a robot!..............

Why, yes, they'll believe you!... Do you want me to go there? I know the police chief!... Okay! See you soon!

Now Madame Adolphine has become a gangster! What a mess!

The police chief is the one who'll be surprised!

POLICE BUREAU

I'm curious to see the look on his face when I tell him about Madame Adolphine!

!

WANTED

CRAZY IVAN

REW
$5...

· NOTICE ·

Hello? Here's little Benny!

Well, now! You caught her! Bravo!

Hey! But-- are you sure that--

Hey, there? What are you doing?

He's taking my pulse! He's obsessed with that!

CRAZY IVAN

REWARD $50,000

Good heavens! You've made a mistake! That's the real Madame Adolphine! Quick! Where's the police chief?

Uh-- in his office! But...

REWARD $50,000

Monsieur Police Chief! You have to release the lady in there! She's not the guilty one!

!?

I'm sorry, my little Benny, but all the witnesses clearly identified her! Isn't that so, Mister Dussiflard?

It's true, Benny! There's no doubt it's really her!

But, no! It looks like her, but it isn't her!

Wait! I'll explain everything to you!...

And two minutes later...

But, yes, it's true!

POLICE CHIEF

--and she did that yesterday because of her reversed circuits! Before that, she was nice!... Like the real one! The one you've arrested and who's not done anything!...

Yes, yes! Now go away and play! I have work to do!

24

--And they didn't believe me! What will we do?

Let's not panic! Madame Adolphine will surely manage to prove she had nothing to do with this matter!

Don't play the innocent, Madame Adolphine! You know full well why you've been arrested!

But no, Mister Police Chief!...

No? Let's see. Think hard! What did you do yesterday? Hmm...?

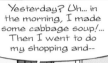

Yesterday? Uh... in the morning, I made some cabbage soup!... Then I went to do my shopping and--

Oh! Yes, now I remember!

Ah-ha! Are you confessing, scoundrel?

Yes, Mister Police Chief! It's true! I crossed the market street even though the light was red!... But I swear to you I won't do it again!

!

It's not about that, for crying out loud! You're accused of armed theft, robbing a bank, and stealing a car!

ME? Is this a joke? Hee hee hee!

No! I advise you to confess right now! **AND STOP LAUGHING!**

Hee hee hee! I beg your pardon, but-- hee hee hee! That's too funny! Hee hee hee!

Later...

And the loot? Where'd you hide the loot?

Where were you on December 13th at 8 o'clock?

We've questioned her for twelve hours, and she still hasn't confessed! She's a tough cookie!

And the taxi?

Do you want some candy?

25

27

Hello? The police station?... Hello, sir! Is Madame Adolphine still being questioned?... No? Really! Did they finally recognize that she was innocent?

WHAT?

They've taken her to prison!

Oh, no! Ask them to connect you to the police chief!

One moment. I'll see if he's there!

Hello? Ah! It's you, Benny... you're still not in bed at this hour?... Yes... no, she didn't confess, but there's no doubt about her guilt!...

Yes, Benny! She has no alibi, and lots of witnesses identified her!... Oh! She'll certainly be sentenced to years in prison...

That's horrible! I assure you she's innocent and that...

Pass him to me!

Hello? Mister police chief? Vladlavodka here! I'm the one who built Madame Adolphine--

--not the one you've arrested, but a robot! Because it's my robot who attacked the bank and--

What?... I- but no, I'm not making fun of-- listen-- sir-- hello-- you--

And I, sir, have only one thing to say to you: remember the infamous miscarriage of justice in the "Courrier de Lyon" case?* --Hello?

He hung up...

Hey! Benny! Where are you going?

To the prison! I'm going to get Madame Adolphine! Wait for me here!

But they won't let you in! Hey! Benny! Come back!

---

* The "Courrier de Lyon" case involved the robbery of a mail coach during the French Revolution. Three men were convicted, but it's believed one was actually innocent. The famous case is remembered as a miscarriage of justice.

A few moments later...

PRISON

Good! Now I have to get inside!

Anybody in sight?...

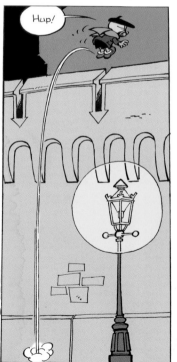

Hup!

And voilà!

Ah! A door!

Everything's going fine so far!... I'm in a little interior courtyard here!

?

AÏE!

Hey, there!

SLAM

Sound the **ALARM!**

An escape?

I've got him, sir! He's there, in the courtyard!

Okay! Go ahead! Open the door!

But-- there's nobody!

No way! It's sorcery!

But there's no way out but this one!

You dreamt it!

But, no, sir, I did see him! He was a little boy with a black beret!

A little boy, eh? Why of course, everyone knows that, at night, prisons are full of little boys with black berets!

But, sir--

Shut up! If this is some joke, it's in poor taste! If it wasn't one, you'd better go see a psychiatrist! Understood?

But really, I swear to you, sir--

⌇Whew!⌇ ... They're gone! That was a close call!

Peyo 28

I'll have to be careful!

And above all, play close attention to not catching a cold! The nights are chilly...

...and this truly would be the worst time to catch a cold!

I don't hear a thing!... Let's go!

Zut! They locked the door shut!

That's annoying! But I have to get in! Too bad, I'll have to force the lock!

KRONK

SCROINK

Nobody? That's good!

Yes, the little old lady they brought us tonight! What's her name again?

Adolphine, sir!

That's it! Well, we'll have to change her cell tomorrow morning!

Put her in eighteen instead of fifteen!...

HEY! YOU THERE!

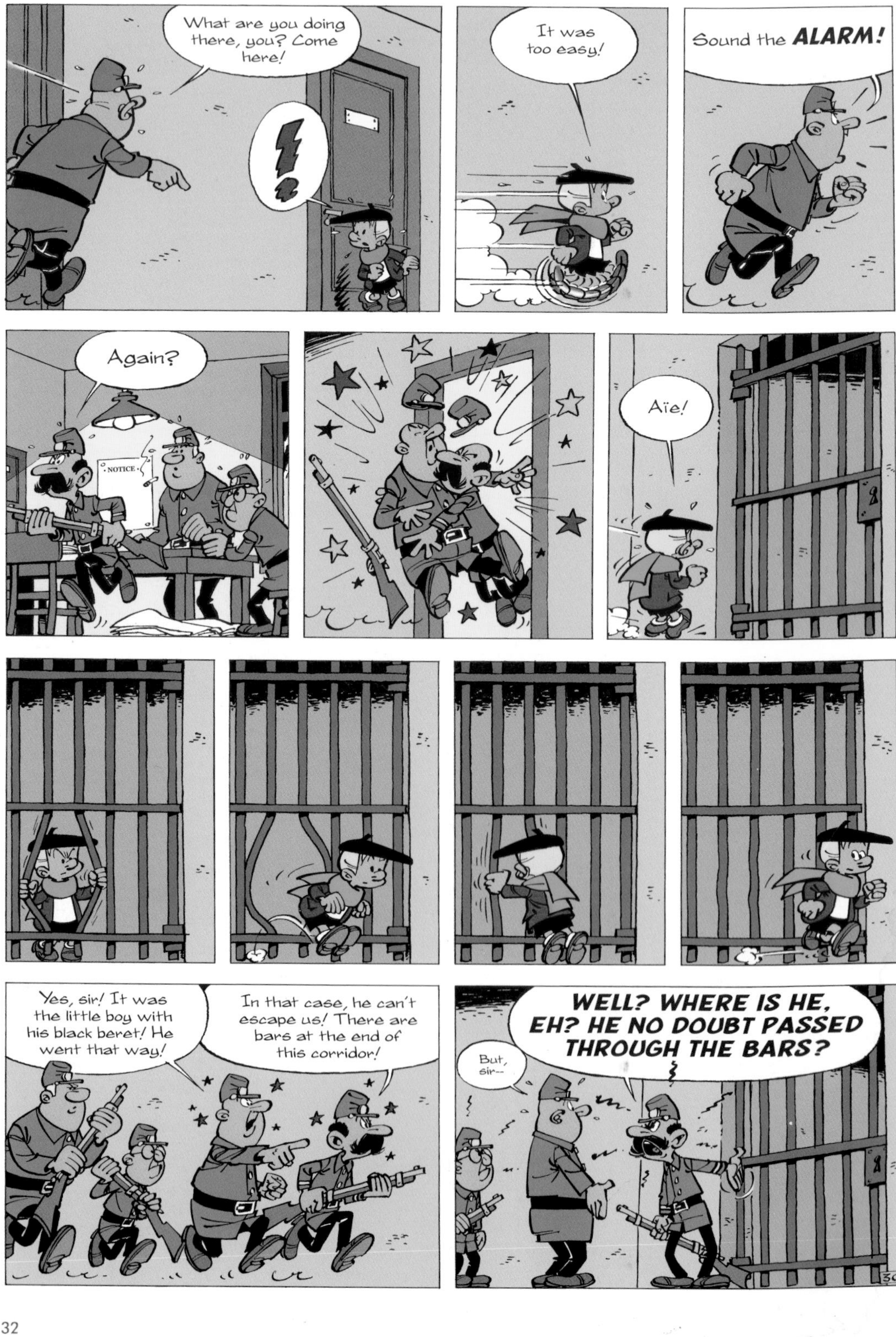
What are you doing there, you? Come here!
It was too easy!
Sound the ALARM!
Again?
Aïe!
Yes, sir! It was the little boy with his black beret! He went that way!
In that case, he can't escape us! There are bars at the end of this corridor!
But, sir--
WELL? WHERE IS HE, EH? HE NO DOUBT PASSED THROUGH THE BARS?
30

Cell number fifteen...

Ah! Here it is!

KROIINK

Don't be frightened, Madame Adolphine, it's me, Benny B--

?

!

Why-- you're not Madame Adolphine?!

No! I'm Julot, known as "Pretty Eyes"! Convicted for theft, abduction, fraud, counterfeiting, extortion... and I forget the rest!

But I heard him well enough! A guard said she was in cell number fifteen!

Well, yeah! In fifteen, in the women's building, no doubt! It's on the other side of the yard! Ha ha ha!

Enough jibber-jabber! Since the door's open, I'm getting away!

!

Ah, no way! You can't! You're a bandit! Go back into your cell!

33

Oh, yeah? Get out of my way, brat, or else--

You're refusing to go back? Too bad...

You asked for it!

POW

And voilà!

CRONK

Now, quickly into the building on the other side of the yard!

No, I wasn't dreaming!... And he did have a black beret!... And if I ever find him, he won't escape me again!...

I'm here! I hope this really is her cell this time!

Who's there?

Ah! That's her! That's her voice!

KROIINK

?

Escape? But Benny, I--

Don't be afraid, everything will be fine! Come quickly!

Most of all, don't make any noise!...

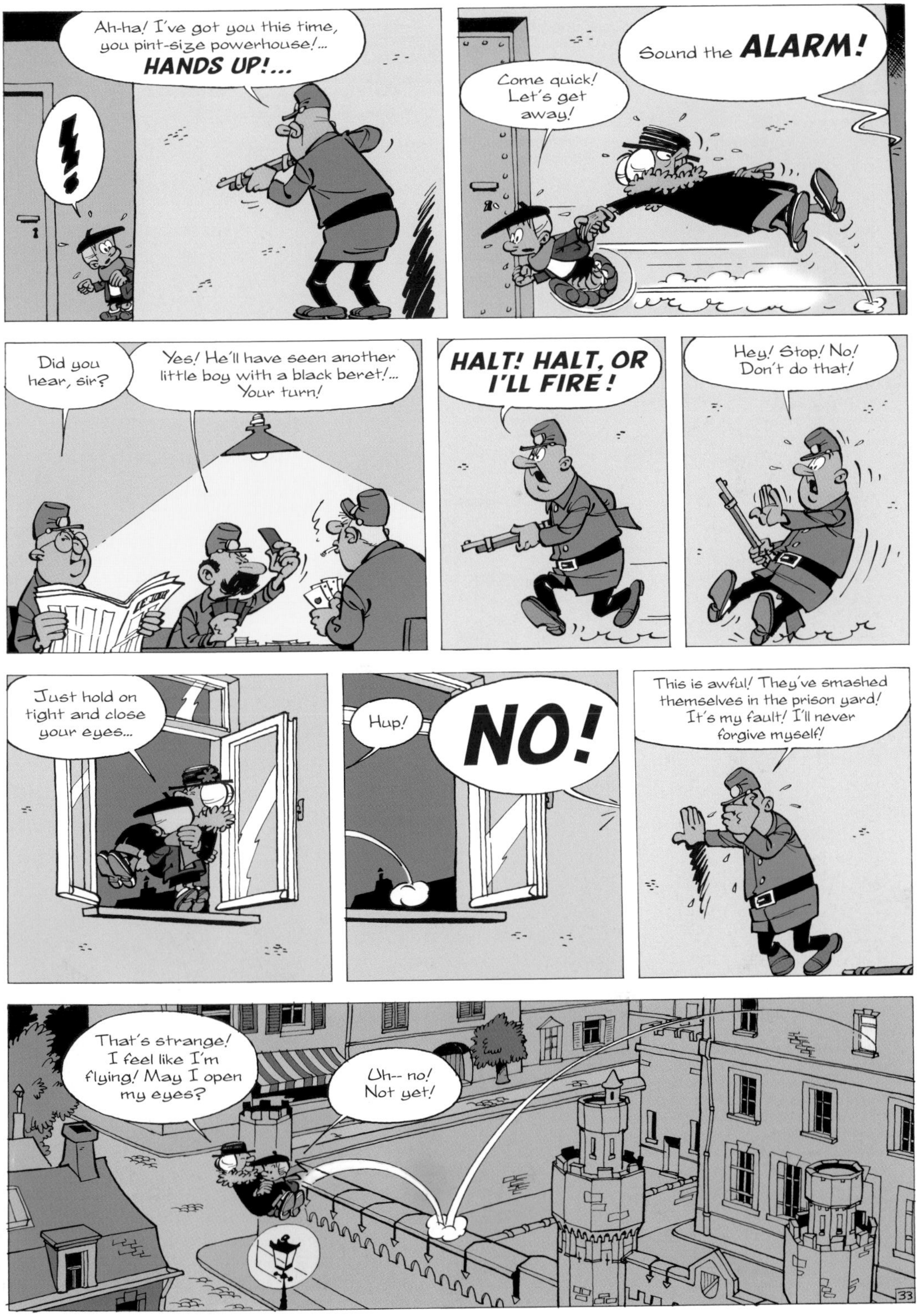

Ah-ha! I've got you this time, you pint-size powerhouse!... HANDS UP!...
Sound the ALARM!
Come quick! Let's get away!
Did you hear, sir?
Yes! He'll have seen another little boy with a black beret!... Your turn!
HALT! HALT, OR I'LL FIRE!
Hey! Stop! No! Don't do that!
Just hold on tight and close your eyes...
Hup!
NO!
This is awful! They've smashed themselves in the prison yard! It's my fault! I'll never forgive myself!
That's strange! I feel like I'm flying! May I open my eyes?
Uh-- no! Not yet!
33

A few moments later...

--and when I opened my eyes, we were on the street!

How is that possible?... What happened?

Uh-- I'll explain it to you later! What's important is that Madame Adolphine is free!

Because now that she's gotten away, the police are going to start pursuing her! And whom will they find? The fake Madame Adolphine! The robot! You understand?

Yes, that's a good idea! What do you think, Madame Adolphine?

Uh-- I'd like that, but I must confess I don't understand anything about this whole story!...

By golly! That's right, you don't know!

We'll explain everything to you...

But, sir, I swear to you they jumped out the window into this yard! It's not my fault they're not here any longer...

A month later...

Oh, Monsieur Vladlavodka! Bonjour!

Hello, Benny!

How's Madame Adolphine?

The real one is fine! She's still hiding out at my place!... The fake one, on the other hand, is continuing her exploits!

Listen to this: "Adolphine, Public Enemy #1, who, sadly, in the last month has made herself infamous through her numerous criminal acts, has just carried out a daring robbery. Yesterday morning, she and her gang attacked and emptied an armored car containing millions of dollars. The police think they have a serious lead."

That's terrible! If only we knew which city she's in...

According to the newspaper, her headquarters are in the capital!

Well, tomorrow, I'll go there! And I'll find her, I swear it!

36

The next day, after an uneventful trip, Benny arrives in the big city...

There're a lot of people! How will I ever find Madame Adolphine?

Excuse me, Monsieur, could you give me some information, please?

Certainly, little boy! Concerning what?

Voilà! I'd like to know where are the bad areas, the slums, the dives where you can find crooks and robbers!

!

You wicked boy! You hoodlum! Aren't you ashamed? Go back home, you gangster, or I'll call for a cop!

But...

Two hours later...

Nobody wants to help me! What will I do?

Go to Chez Juju's! It's a cafe! Second street on the left!

Merci!

Second street on the left! Chez Juju's!

Ah! Here is it!

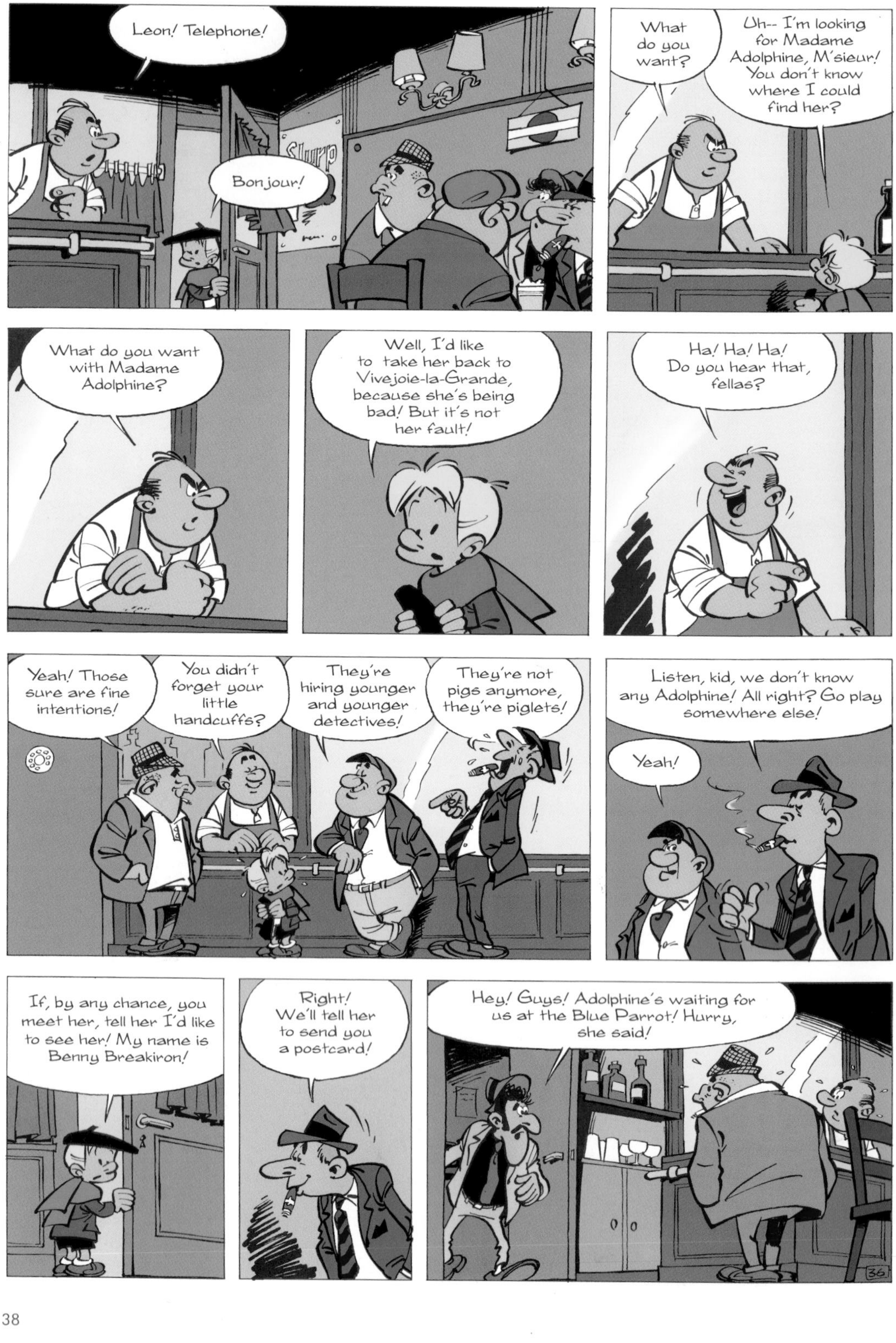
Leon! Telephone!
Bonjour!
What do you want?
Uh-- I'm looking for Madame Adolphine, M'sieur! You don't know where I could find her?
What do you want with Madame Adolphine?
Well, I'd like to take her back to Vivejoie-la-Grande, because she's being bad! But it's not her fault!
Ha! Ha! Ha! Do you hear that, fellas?
Yeah! Those sure are fine intentions!
You didn't forget your little handcuffs?
They're hiring younger and younger detectives!
They're not pigs anymore, they're piglets!
Listen, kid, we don't know any Adolphine! All right? Go play somewhere else!
Yeah!
If, by any chance, you meet her, tell her I'd like to see her! My name is Benny Breakiron!
Right! We'll tell her to send you a postcard!
Hey! Guys! Adolphine's waiting for us at the Blue Parrot! Hurry, she said!
36

So you **DO** know Madame Adolphine...

Where's the "Blue Parrot"?

What? You're still here?... Wait, you pipsqueak, we'll teach you to spy on us!

HEY! GET BACK HERE!

Well, I didn't know that kid was there!

Should've paid attention! ©!☆7⛧⚡○?

Catch him! He knows too much!

Quick! To the car!

Hee hee! They can keep on running, they can't catch me now!

Excuse me, M'sieur Police Officer, where's the "Blue Parrot"?

First left, second right! Pass the bridge and continue straight ahead! At the second red light, take the boulevard on the right, and it's a hundred yards away! You can't--

Miss it...

Merci, M'sieur!

Blast it! There's no hope of finding him! We better go warn Adolphine!

You're in big trouble, Leon!

But--

22 X 157

37

39

A few moments later...

That's it!

Whoa, young man, you're not allowed to come in here! This is a private club!

Go get Madame Adolphine for me! I know she's here!

What? That gangster woman? Here, at the "Blue Parrot"? Is that a joke?

Know, my little friend, that this club includes in its membership only decent folk! And now, get out or else I'll call the police!

Uh-- I-- I must be mistaken! I misheard! Excuse me!

THERE HE IS!

We got him!

So, kid, trying to give us the slip?

That's not nice!

He deserves a spanking from us!

Don't you touch me! You better watch out! I'm strong! I warn you, I could beat up all of you!

Ha! Ha! Ha! That's a good one!

I'm scared!

What's all the commotion? What's going on here?

Madame Adolphine!

My goodness! Why it's little Benny!...

How you doing, kid? It's been ages since we last saw each other!

Come, let's drink to that! Ernest! A bottle of hard stuff! Get a move on!

She's talking as bad as ever!

So? What did you come to do in the city?

I came looking for you to take you back to Vivejoie-la-Grande!

Ha! Ha! Are you kidding? But tell me, who told you I was here?

Not me!

It's him!

Yeah! It's Leon!

Uh... I can explain, Madame Adolphine...

Explain? Explain what? Huh? You moron! I'll make you regret that!

If the cops start nosing around, I'll buy you a pine box! Get it?

Why, I ought to-- to--

?

Madame Adolphine! What's wrong? Are you all right?

39

41

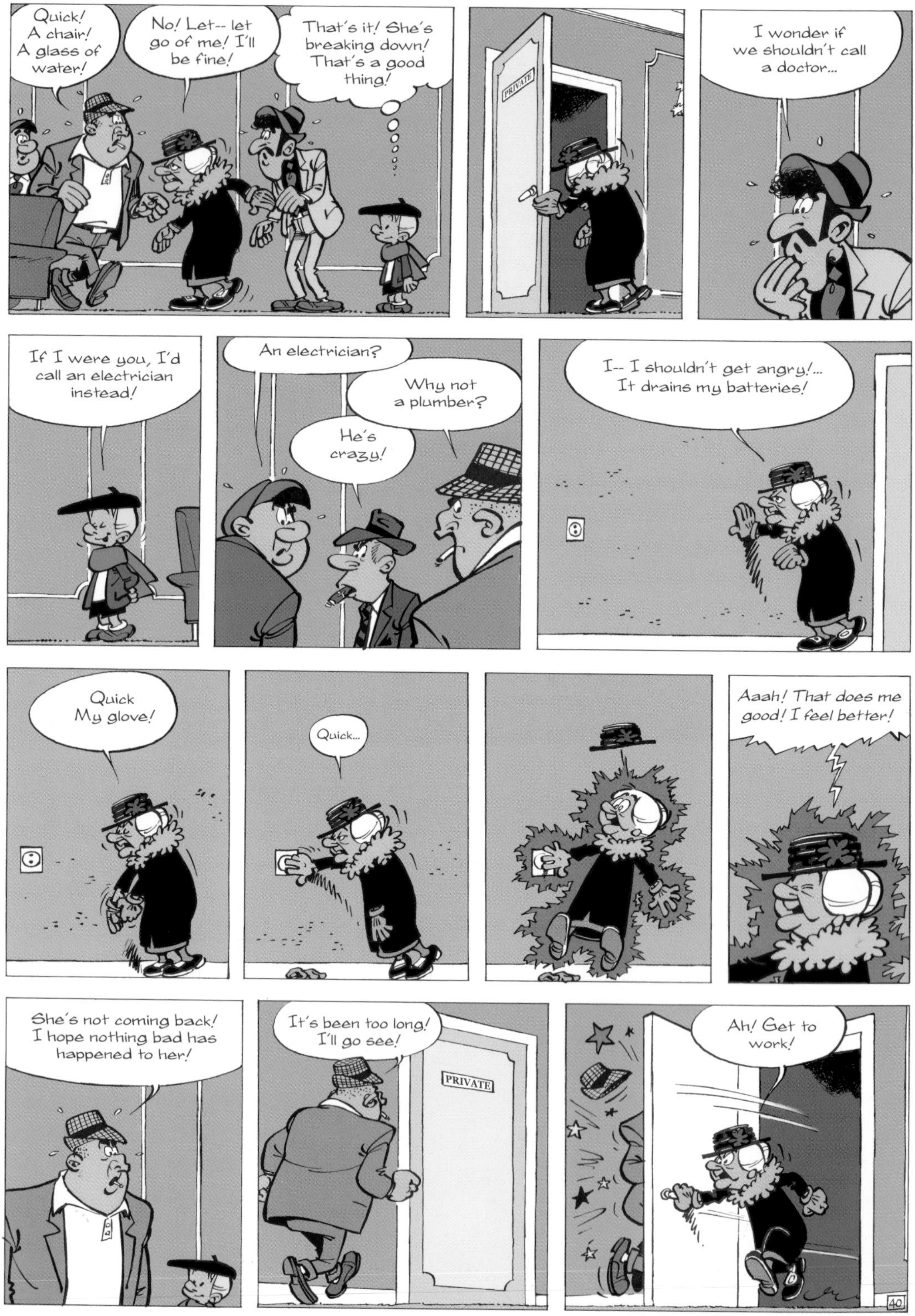
Quick! A chair! A glass of water!
No! Let-- let go of me! I'll be fine!
That's it! She's breaking down! That's a good thing!
PRIVATE
I wonder if we shouldn't call a doctor...
If I were you, I'd call an electrician instead!
An electrician?
Why not a plumber?
He's crazy!
I-- I shouldn't get angry!... It drains my batteries!
Quick My glove!
Quick...
Aaah! That does me good! I feel better!
She's not coming back! I hope nothing bad has happened to her!
It's been too long! I'll go see!
PRIVATE
Ah! Get to work!
40

Listen closely! We're going to rob the mint! Everything's ready to go! I got the truck! The costumes are in the next room! So get dressed and be quick about it!

What happened? She seemed all out of whack?

Madame Adolphine, excuse me! You absolutely must return to Vivejoie-la-Grande!

Of course, Benny, of course!

Say, Madame Adolphine...

?

Do we really have to wear this?

PRIVATE

You bunch of nitwits! You've put on the outfits to be used for the costume party! Go put on the **OVERALLS!**

Such imbeciles! Now they've made me mad again! They'll end up ruining my batteries!

So, are you coming? Say...

And none too soon! Go on! Get going! I'll follow you in the car!

And the kid? What do we do with him?

He knows too much! We'll take him along! Let's go!

Where are we going? Vivejoie?

No! Later!

VACUUMALL

For now, we're going to clean out the mint!

Oh? You clean up buildings?

And why not, my boy? All work is honorable, isn't it?

Ah! We're here! Wait for me, it'll be over quick!

Here? What a funny hotel!

Are you ready? Okay! Let's go!

Hey! What is this-- who are you?

We're the "Vacuumall" company, we do vacuum dust removal! The finance office asked us to come clean the building!

Ah? In that case, you must have an official authorization?

Certainly! I'll show it to you!

Here! Here's my official authorization! Go on! Lead us to the machines that make the coins! And no fooling around or else--

!

A cleaning business is honest work! Maybe, deep down, Madame Adolphine isn't so bad after all!

Hands up! Everyone face the wall!

42

Tie those guys up for me! You, Leon, turn the vacuum on and get to work!

DINGALING TCHING KLING DING DI

DINGALING KLING CHING DINGA

There are no more dimes, but here are some quarters!

I'll see to the small change!

And bingo! Another bucket empty!

This works really well!

And a few moments later...

That's it! There isn't a penny left!

Good! Come on! We're out of here!

You go park the van at the garage! I'll get rid of the kid! We'll meet at the "Blue Parrot"!

Already done?

Yes! It's all cleaned out!

45

Where are we going now?

The train station!

We're going to see when there's a train for Vivejoie-la-Grande!

Cool! She's decided to come back! We'll be able to prove the real Madame Adolphine is innocent!

Step on it! There's one in five minutes!

Quick! A ticket for Vivejoie-la-Grande!

Hey! Wait! You made a mistake! You only got one ticket!

Well, yes, it's for you!

What? You're not coming with me? Ah! Well, no... in that case, I'm not leaving either!

Listen, kid, I can't just run off like that! Uh-- first of all, I've got to close down my cleaning business! I'll come afterwards!

When.....? Tomorrow?

That's right! Tomorrow!

You'll come, won't you? Promise?

I swear!

Bye!

All right!

44

A little later, the train plunges into the night, carrying Benny towards Vivejoie-la-Grande...

Ah! We're almost there...!

I wonder if I was right to trust Madame Adolphine...

These are our headlines!

This afternoon, a bold hold-up was committed in the mint by Adolphine's gang. Disguised as workers from a cleaning company, the bandits--

!

-- literally vacuumed up hundreds of thousands of dollars in coins! In New York--

She really fooled me!...

But this isn't how it's going to go! I'm going back there!

?

Pardon me!

Sapristi! Why, that man is the prison guard!

Why-- that's the little boy who--

Hey! Come here!

Quick! The door!

Hey! No! Don't-- don't do that!

NO!

47

It's awful! That's the second time he's killed himself because of me!

ALARM

÷Whew!÷ And now, to get back on track!

She won't fool me again this time! I'll take her back to Vivejoie-la-Grande willingly **OR BY FORCE!**

POSTE 8

!?

An hour later...
Why no, I don't have hallucinations! He was a little boy with a black beret--

II

II

And meanwhile...
There's the city! I'll have to find the "Blue Parrot" again!

Ah! There it is!
PRIVATE CLUB
HOTEL DU COMMERCE

Blue Parrot
Just the two of us now, Madame Adolphine!
PRIVATE CLUB

48

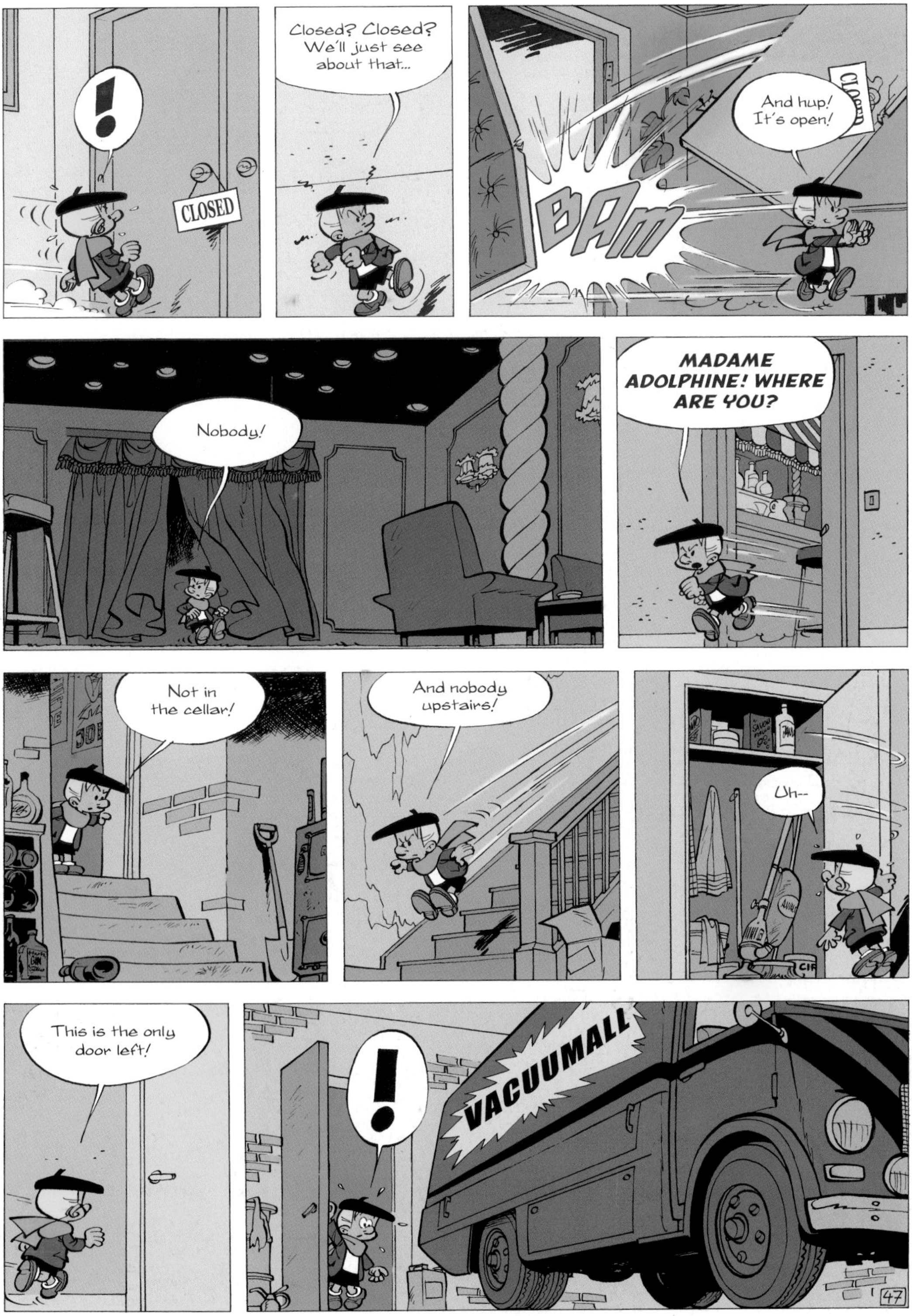
!
CLOSED
Closed? Closed? We'll just see about that...
CLOSED
BAM
And hup! It's open!
Nobody!
MADAME ADOLPHINE! WHERE ARE YOU?
Not in the cellar!
And nobody upstairs!
Uh--
This is the only door left!
!
VACUUMALL
47

Why, that's the truck they used to do the hold-up! I wonder if--

Yes! The coins are still there! Good! Well, I know what I'm going to do!

VACUU

Raise the garage door first!

Next...

Hup!

And away we go!

VACUUMALL

Luckily the streets are deserted at this hour!

Sapristi! I'm so hungry! With all this fuss, I've not eaten since this morning!

VACUUMALL

Hey! Oh! Stop!

A candy machine! That's lucky!

Zut! I don't have any money on me!

No money? Heh heh! The truck's full of it!

Why, that's right!

48

50

Ah! No way! I can't! That money isn't mine!

Bah! Just one little coin! Nobody will ever know!

No! It wouldn't be right! What's more, just like my teacher says, "give an inch and he'll take a mile"!

‡Pff!‡ That's a joke!

Come on, go ahead! There's milk chocolate with hazelnuts! Just like you like! Chocolate is good, yum yum!

POW

There are so many bad, little boys on earth, and I had to be **BENNY BREAKIRON's** guilty conscience!

VACUUMALL

A few minutes later...

Ah! There's the mint!

DRIIIIDRIIIING

?

BOOM BOOM BOOM

What is it? What do you want?

I came to return to you the money that Madame Adolphine stole from you! It's all there in the truck!

Voilà! Bonsoir, M'sieur!

What? But— but—

Oh! Oh! It's starting to rain!

I'm wasting my time here! I have to find Madame Adolphine... or her accomplices!

That's just it! Where are they?... Maybe at the little café where I met them that morning?...

Chez Juju!

What a downpour! I'm wet to the bone!

That's their car!

So we meet again, eh?

Little Benny?!

But-- I thought he was gone!

Where's Madame Adolphine?... Come on, answer! And don't try to trick me or you'd better look out!

No kidding, you're starting to get on our nerves, kid! We're going to lock you in the basement, that way you won't annoy us anymore!

Ah! Don't try it! I've already told you: I'm very strong!

Oh, yeah! Ha! Ha! Ha! Go ahead! Show me your strength! Go on, hit me!

Okay! You asked for it

POW

VITTEL DÉLICES

BONK

南!?

Lower the shutters, Juju! There's going to be a fistfight!

50

52

I got him!

Hey! I didn't do anything! Help!

You see I'm strong!... Well? Where's Madame Adolphine?

Open up!

51

53

Who's there?

It's me, Adolphine! Raise this shutter! And fast!

Voilà! Voilà!

What happened here? Did you beat each other up?

Slurp

Come on, get up G!☆※ This isn't the time for napping! The truck with all the loot got stolen! We have to find the guy who did a number on us!

?

Don't look far! It's me!

Benny?! But what are you doing here? I thought you were in Vivejoie-la-Grande!

Uh... no.

Ah?... Uh, so you're the one who took the truck? I'm glad! Where'd you ditch it?

I took it back to the mint!

What? Are you crazy? You little brat, I'm going to give you a spanking you'll never forget!

No! Don't do that, Madame Adolphine!

He's awful strong!

What are you talking about? Let me go!

She was just going for a laugh, Mister Benny!

You don't believe me, eh? Well, look at this chair!...

You'll see what I can do! I – ah... ah... ah...

ATCHOOO!

52

Oh, no! That's it! I have a cold! I must have caught it just now in the rain! And now I've lost all my strength!

What, then? Are you deciding?

Go ahead, little guy! Show Madame Adolphine what you're going to do with that chair!

Watch closely!

What-- what I'm going to do? Uh-- hmm! I--

⇥Umpf!⇤

Voilà!

My, my, boys, I don't much like when someone's pulling my leg!

We're wasting our time here! We've got to try to get the truck back **ASAP!**

Here, take this, Juju, and lock the kid up in your basement! I'll deal with him later!

Come on! Get a move on!

Where are we going?

To the "Blue Parrot"! Step on it!

It was too good to be true!

53

55

I don't understand! That kid has extraordinary strength! He breaks everything! And then he lets himself be locked in the basement!... I don't get it!

I have to get out of here! But how? So long as I have this blasted cold, I can't do anything!

HONK

Meanwhile, I'm as hungry as ever!

BOOM BOOM BOOM

?

What is it?

I'm hungry! Could you bring me something to eat?

Uh-- okay! But you behave, eh?

I promise!

And meanwhile...

PRIVATE CLUB

Quick!

There! Don't even budge!

My goodness, you've caught a nasty cold!

ATCHOOO

Yes! I'll have to take care of myself!... and take medicine!

SNIF

Ah?... It's just that I don't have any here!

That's okay!... Provided I don't catch broncho-pneumonia in this damp cellar! I already feel feverish!... Ah! If only I had some medicine!

And now on to the mint!

PRIVATE CLUB

54

56

Just think, for lack of care, I may have to spend the rest of my life in a hospital bed dreaming about my little friends playing without me at the Jules Petty Square!

No! Wait! I'll go find you some medicine! I-- I'll be right back!

A pharmacy! Quick! A pharmacy!

Meanwhile...

It's just what I thought! The police have already been alerted, and they sent two cops to guard the truck!... Okay! You know what you have to do! Get going!

Hello? There's our back-up!

Hi! We came to get the truck to drive it to a safe location!

Ah?... Uh-- it's just I don't know if I can!... Who sent you? I've never seen you before!

Of course! We're the secret police!

Ah? But why are you in uniform then?

Shh! It's a ruse! With this disguise, nobody will ever think we're the secret police! Do you understand?

Uh--

I was also telling myself they don't look like real officers!

Let's get on our way!

VACUUMALL

$⑤!?☆※$ What? Are you kidding me? Waking me up in the middle of the night for a cold?

But it's a big cold!

55

He's taking his time! And Madame Adolphine could come back any moment now!

Ah! I hear someone!

There! I got everything I could find! If we don't cure your cold with this...

!

♪ Pass the money, Pass the money, move it around... ♫

VACUUMALL

...Ten... eleven... twelve! There! Quickly drink this while I prepare an inhalation for you! Afterwards, I'll put some drops in your nose! Do you have a temperature? How do you feel?

Hmm!

I feel better! I think that I-- I--

ATCHOOO

Secret police? Secret police? You blithering idiots! ©!?⚡ You let yourself be fooled like children!

That's another stunt by Adolphine's gang! We have to catch them! **HELLO!**

OOOOEEEOOCCCEEEEEEE CCCCCCCCCC

POLICE

!

Take it slow! All right! You're through!

CUUMALL

VROOM VROOM

56

x

58

Okay! Go get dressed again! We're going back to *Chez Juju!* I have a score to settle with that Benny kid!

There!... Now rub some camphorated alcohol on yourself while I make you a nice, hot toddy!

BOOM BOOM BOOM

Uh-oh! That's Adolphine! Wait! I'll go open the door for her!

Aïe! I'm doomed!

Quick! There's still some medicine I haven't taken!

POP

CHIF CHIF CHIF

This is my last chance!

CLUC CLUC CLUC

SCRUNCH

CRUNCH

⇉Pfff!⇇ And now let's try to bend this iron bar! If my cold is cured, I ought to...

Ha! Ha! Now it's just you and me, boy!

No, he didn't do anything to me! He was nice even!

That's amazing! Maybe he's lost his strength!

That's possible! In that case, I worry what Adolphine must be doing to him!

AAAH! HELP ME! HELP!

There we go! I bent it! I'm cured!

And it's thanks to you! Merci, M'sieur Juju!

?

joy

And now, it's just you and me, Madame Adolphine!

57

Ay-yi-yi!

He's gotten strong again!

He's going to beat us up again!

No! Mercy!

The police!

We're safe!

?

Don't come any closer or else-- careful, watch out! You've been warned!

Ah! He nicked my piece! Give it back!

Why, yes! I'll give it back to you tout de suite!

GRAB SRSOVCH

Here you go!

Enough kidding around! You got the truck back, eh? Where is it?

Uh-- in the "Blue Parrot's" garage!

Good! Follow me!

And a few moments later...

VACUUMALL   VACUUMALL

VROOM

And now to the mint!

58

60

What? Someone-- someone returned the truck to you?... But who?... A little boy and an old lady?... And where are they?... Gone?... Why this story will drive me mad!

And the next morning in Vivejoie-la-Grande...

So there, Mr. Police Chief, the proof that Madame Adolphine is innocent!

Here's the guilty one! She's my robot!

Ah! Sorry! You're mistaken! I'm Madame Adolphine!

What? That's not true! It's me!

My goodness! What cheek!

She's an imposter!

Usurper!

Machine yourself!

You've got some nerve!

Liar!

Dumb machine!

Uh-- let's see, ladies. I-- good heavens! Which one's the real one?

Wait! There's a simple way to find out!

This one's the robot! She has no pulse!

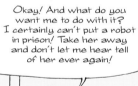

⑥!?⚡

Okay! And what do you want me to do with it? I certainly can't put a robot in prison! Take her away and don't let me hear tell of her ever again!

And there! Everything's settled!

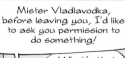
Mister Vladlavodka, before leaving you, I'd like to ask you permission to do something!

What's that, Madame Adolphine?

THIS!

POW

!

I beg your pardon, but I couldn't help it! That awful robot did me so much harm!

61

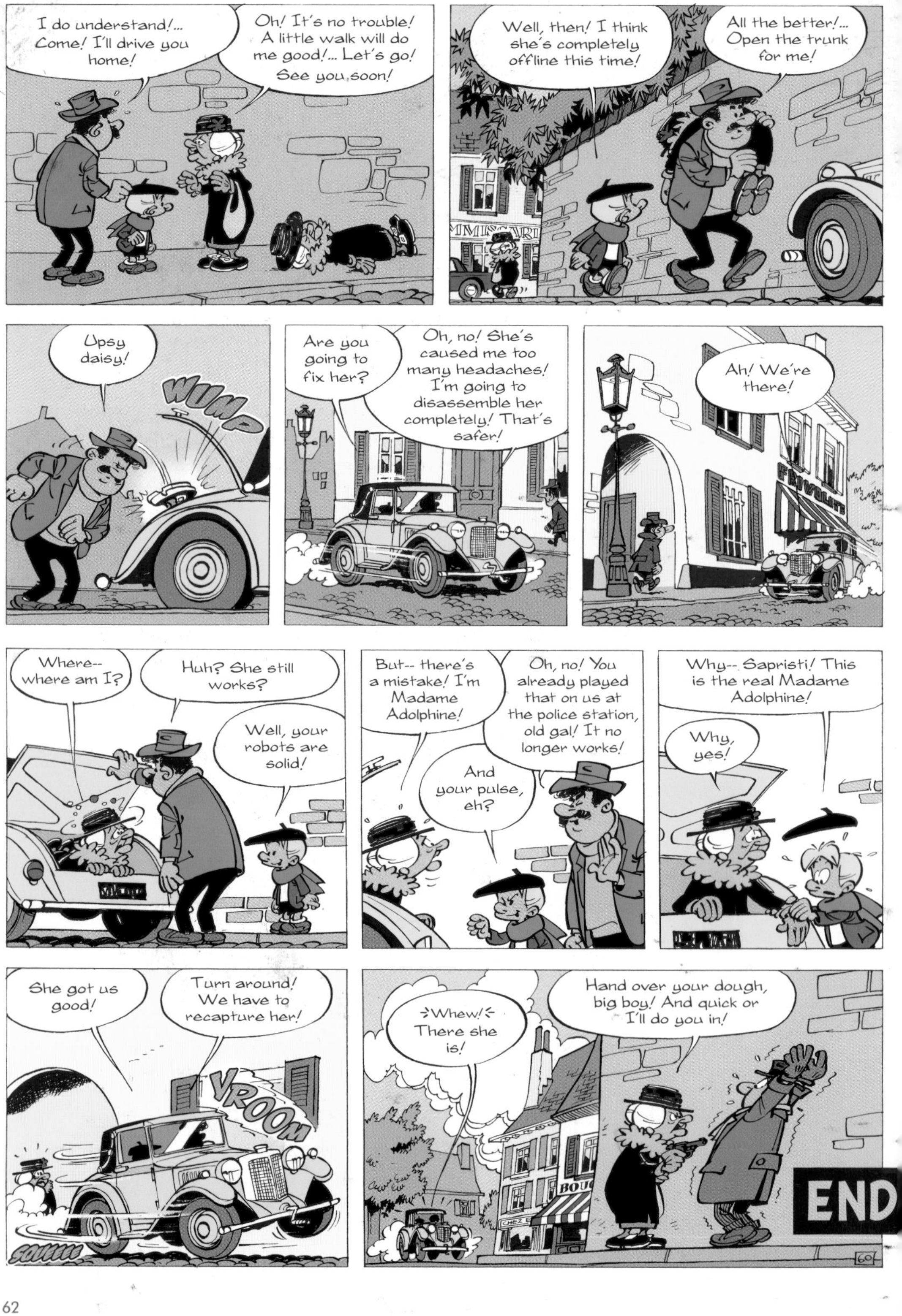
I do understand!... Come! I'll drive you home!
Oh! It's no trouble! A little walk will do me good!... Let's go! See you soon!
Well, then! I think she's completely offline this time!
All the better!... Open the trunk for me!
Upsy daisy!
WUMP
Are you going to fix her?
Oh, no! She's caused me too many headaches! I'm going to disassemble her completely! That's safer!
Ah! We're there!
FRIVOLITE
Where-- where am I?
Huh? She still works?
Well, your robots are solid!
But-- there's a mistake! I'm Madame Adolphine!
Oh, no! You already played that on us at the police station, old gal! It no longer works!
And your pulse, eh?
Why-- Sapristi! This is the real Madame Adolphine!
Why, yes!
She got us good!
Turn around! We have to recapture her!
VROOM
Whew! There she is!
Hand over your dough, big boy! And quick or I'll do you in!
END

WATCH OUT FOR PAPERCUTZ™

Welcome to the super-powered, cybernetic, stuck-in-the-sixties, second BENNY BREAKIRON graphic novel by Peyo from Papercutz. We're the itty-bitty comics company dedicated to publishing great graphic novels for all ages. That, of course, includes the wondrous works of Pierre Culliford, better known as Peyo. We're proud to be publishing THE SMURFS, *Johan and Peewit* (now featured in THE SMURFS ANTHOLOGY), and of course, BENNY BREAKIRON, that pint-sized powerhouse.

I'm Jim Salicrup, the Editor-in-Chief and Asker of Silly Questions. For example, did anyone notice I got the year wrong in BENNY BREAKIRON #1, when I wrote that Benny "first appeared in 1962"? Yes! Our very own resident Smurf Consultant, Matt. Murray, was the first to point out that Benny Breakiron (or *Benoît Brisefer*, as he was originally dubbed) actually appeared in issue 1183 of *Spirou* magazine in mid-December, 1960. We'll be sure to correct that little flub in future printings of BENNY BREAKIRON #1.

Another interesting tidbit about BENNY BREAKIRON #1 is the cover. A little over 25 years ago, to celebrate the 50th anniversary of Superman, the hero who inspired all other super-heroes, I thought it would be clever to pay homage to the cover of ACTION COMICS #1, where Superman first debuted. I was editing THE AMAZING SPIDER-MAN at that time, so Todd McFarlane drew a great tribute cover of Spidey lifting a police car. I thought I was so clever--I thought no one had ever done that before! Well, you can imagine my surprise when I saw this--the original cover for *Benoît Brisefer*:

Peyo published his tribute to ACTION COMICS #1 almost 30 years before we did! So, now that so many other comics are running their ACTION COMICS #1 cover tributes, I find it very amusing, but not surprising, to discover that Peyo did it first!

Hey, this is fun! Let's meet again in BENNY BREAKIRON #3 "The Twelve Trials of Benny Breakiron," where we'll talk more about the genius of Peyo, okay?

Merci,

Jim

"The characters that I've created are not tough guys at the outset. They become strong together, by being united."

— PEYO

Over 50 years ago, a Belgian cartoonist known as Peyo set his pencil to a blank page and created a worldwide phenomenon we know as The Smurfs. Join us in celebrating more than a half century of humor, camaraderie, heroism, and heart. Experience the master at his best.

THE WONDER OF PEYO

INCOMPARABLE NEW GRAPHIC NOVELS FROM PAPERCUT℠

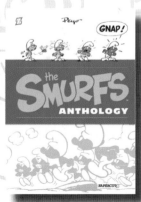

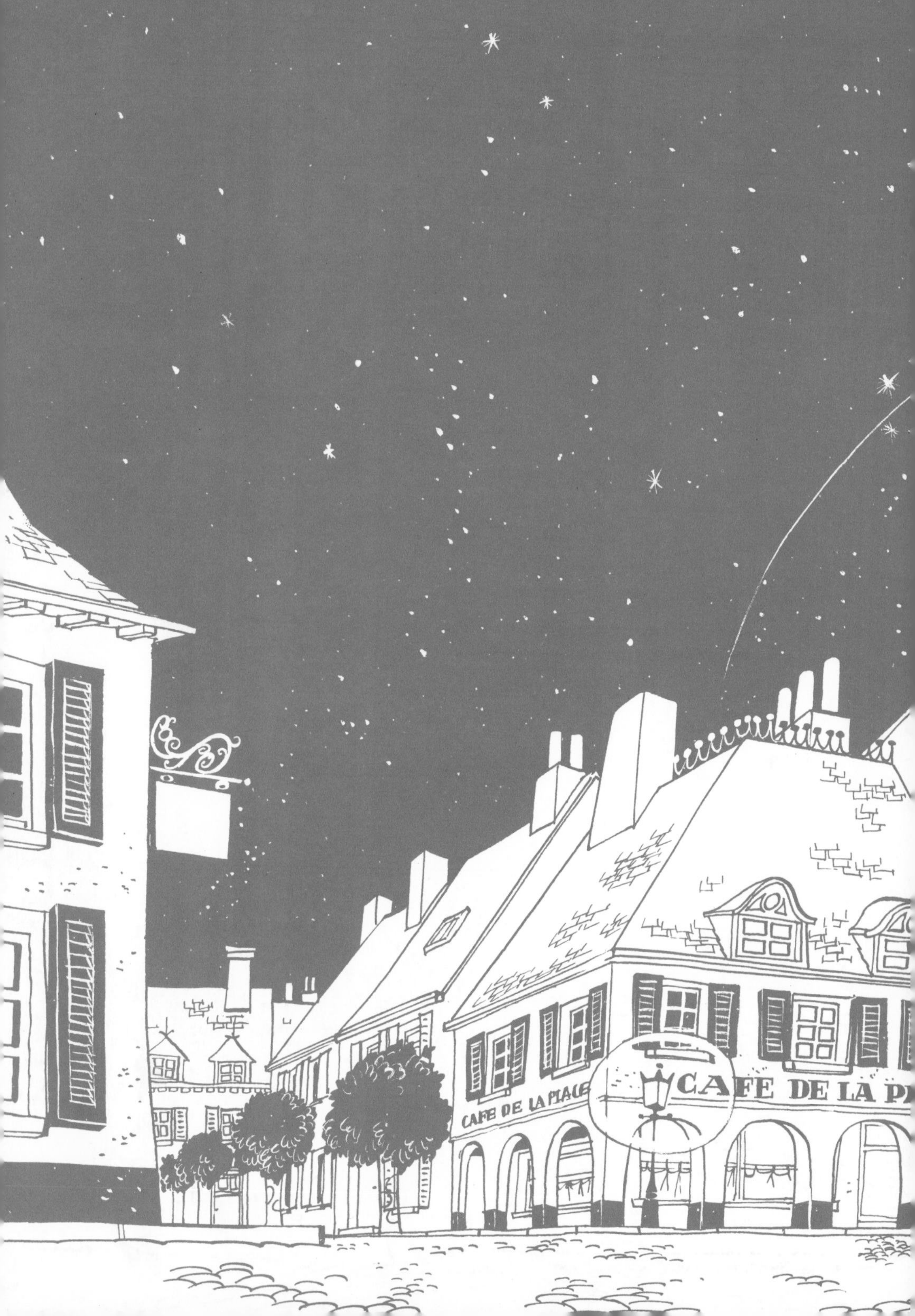
CAFE DE LA PLACE
CAFE DE LA P